SHARON JENNINGS

A Home for Us

ILLUSTRATED BY

EVA CAMPBELL

Red Deer Press

Published in Canada by Red Deer Press, 195 Allstate Parkway, Markham, ON L3R 4T8
Published in the United States by Red Deer Press, 311 Washington Street, Brighton, MA 02135

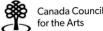 

Red Deer Press acknowledges with thanks the Canada Council for the Arts and the Ontario Arts Council for their support of our publishing program. We acknowledge the financial support of the Government of Canada through the Canada Book Fund (CBF) for our publishing activities.

Library and Archives Canada Cataloguing in Publication

Title: A Home for us / Sharon Jennings ; illustrations by Eva Campbell.
Names: Jennings, Sharon, 1954- author. | Campbell, Eva, illustrator.
Description: First edition.
Identifiers: Canadiana 20210296437 | ISBN 9780889955752 (hardcover)
Classification: LCC PS8567.E563 H63 2022 | DDC jC813/.54—dc23

Publisher Cataloging-in-Publication Data (U.S.)

Names: Jennings, Sharon, 1954-, author. | Campbell, Eva, illustrator.
Title: A Home for Us / Sharon Jennings ; illustrations by Eva Campbell.
Description: Markham, Ontario : Red Deer Press, 2022. | Summary: "A Home for Us is a realistic fiction picture book about a little girl named Yula—an orphan who is discovered living alone and brought to live at the Hope Development Centre in Kikima, Kenya. This orphanage is a real place, visited by author Sharon Jennings who was inspired to create this story about the importance of home and family" – Provided by publisher.
Identifiers: ISBN 978-0-88995-575-2 (hardcover)
Subjects: LCSH: Orphans – Juvenile fiction. | Families – Juvenile fiction. | Orphanages – Juvenile fiction. | Hope Development Centre (Kenya) – Juvenile fiction.| BISAC: JUVENILE NONFICTION / Family / Orphans & Foster Homes. | JUVENILE FICTION / Family / Orphans & Foster Homes
Classification: LCC PZ7.J466Hom | DDC 813.6 – dc23

The illustrations are done in gouache, acrylic and ink on canvas.
Edited for the Press by Beverley Brenna
Text and cover design by Kong Njo
Printed in Hong Kong, China by Sheck Wah Tong Printing

www.reddeerpress.com

Many thanks to Eric and Anita Walters
for introducing me to Ruth and Henry
and the children of
Hope Development Centre
in Kikima, Kenya

—S. J.

To my uncle Samuel Asihene
and my nephew Gabriel

—E. C.

Sharon is a greatly welcomed, and return visitor to Hope Development Centre in Kikima, Kenya. The children and staff enjoy her visits and we consider her a member of our Hope family. During one of her visits, she met a child who inspired her to write *A Home For Us*. The story has been shared with our children and they love it! We have not only given Sharon our permission but our thanks to her for telling this story. We are pleased that she is donating a portion of her royalties to our program to support the orphaned and impoverished children of Hope.   —RUTH KYATHA

Yula is maybe four. Mother and father are late.
She lies on ground with goat. Hungry.
Always hungry.
She cannot walk. She cannot talk.
"Orphan," says stranger.

Stranger wraps Yula in blanket.

   She says, "We will go in a car to a hospital."
What is go? What is car? What is hospital?

   Gentle hands search her body. *What is
ringworm? What is malnutrition?*

   She curls up on soft. Not hard. Not dirt.
Not ground. "Bed," says stranger.

   Will she fall?

Stranger brings a bowl and spoon. "Soup," she says.

Yula swallows again and again and again.

Stranger points to herself. "Mum," she says. "I am called Mum."

Alone in bed. "Mum," Yula whispers. "Mum-mum-mum-mum-mum."

Light.

Mum puts her arm around Yula.

"I will teach you to walk," she says.

What is walk?

Yula sits down. Ground is safe.

Light and dark, light and dark,

light and dark. Walk, walk, walk.

And spoon and swallow.

"Mum," says Yula.

Mum smiles and hugs Yula.

Car again. "We are going to my orphanage," Mum says.

What is orphanage?

Car drives up, up, up the hills. Bump, bump, bump.

Car stops. Big house. Mum spreads her arms wide. "This is my home," says Mum. "Now it is your home, too."

Small strangers shout, "Hello, Yula!"

Yula cries and hides face in Mum's skirt.

"Shhh, shhh," says Mum, hugging Yula.

Dark and light. Light and dark. Over and over. Many walks with Mum. Mum points. "Bananas," she says. "Too green to eat. One day, they will be ready for us."

Points. "Mangos," she says. "Too small to eat. One day, they will be ready for us."

Points. "Sunflowers," she says. "Not ready to blossom. One day, they will be ready for us."

"But the cow is ready to give us milk,"
says Mum. "And the chicken is ready to
give us eggs."

Yula wonders, what is *us*?

Many darks and lights. Another walk. Down, down, down the hill. Mum points. "School," she says. She points to new stranger. "Teacher," she says.

"Hello, Yula," says Teacher.

Every light she goes to school. One light she points to herself. "Yula," she says.

The children cheer and clap.

One light Mum gets in car with suitcase and waves. "Bye-bye," Mum says. Yula cries and chases car. "It is alright, Yula," Teacher says. "Mum will come back to us."

Light and dark. At school, Yula learns this is called a day. Yula counts seven, and this is a week. Four weeks and this is a month.

Yula plays and sings and learns and eats and prays and sleeps with others. Others are all like Yula. Mothers and fathers are late.

Others are all orphans, too.

One month and two days. Yula hears car and runs with others. Mum holds onto little boy. "This is Mutuku," Mum says. "He is maybe three. Mother and father are late."

The children shout, "Hello, Mutuku!"

Yula shouts, too. "My mum!" She pushes Mutuku. "Go away!"

Mutuku cries and hides face in Mum's skirt.

Teacher holds Yula, but Yula hits and runs fast.

Yula hides in field.

"Yula! Yula!" Everyone calls her name.

Yula stays silent.

"Yula! Yula!"

Sun down. Light gone. Yula sneaks to goat pen. Sleep doesn't come. Thoughts come. Now others are praying, Yula thinks. Now they are eating beans and maize and chapati. Now they are singing, they are washing, they are sleeping in soft beds with each other, not on hard ground with old goat.

They are together in house with Mum.

Yula shivers. She remembers cold and dark.
Tummy is empty. Yula remembers hungry.
Something howls. Yula remembers afraid.
Yula remembers alone.

Rooster crows. Yula wakes and climbs over fence. Sun rises up, up, up.

In garden, mangoes are plump and bananas are yellow. In field, sunflowers are open.

"Mum!" Yula shouts. "Everything is ready! Everything is ready for us, Mum!"

Mum comes running. All the children come running. "Yula! Yula!" they call. Everyone hugs Yula.

Mum bends down. She looks into Yula's eyes. "Is Yula ready for us?"

Yula knows the answer. She smiles. "Today, I am ready for us."

Yula hugs Mutuku. "This is my home,"
she tells him. "Now it is your home, too."
She smiles. "This is a home for us."